Mog and Bunny

JUDITH KERR

Alfred A. Knopf · New York

For Lucy and Alexander

This is a Borzoi Book published by Alfred A. Knopf, Inc.

Text and illustrations copyright © 1988 by Kerr-Kneale Productions Ltd. All rights reserved under International and Pan-American Copyright Conventions. Published in the United States by Alfred A. Knopf, Inc., New York. Distributed by Random House, Inc., New York. Originally published in Great Britain by William Collins Sons & Co. Ltd., London, in 1988. First American Edition, 1989. Manufactured in Great Britain   1 2 3 4 5 6 7 8 9 0

Library of Congress Cataloging-in-Publication Data
Kerr, Judith. Mog and Bunny / Judith Kerr.—1st American ed.   p.   cm. Summary: The family threatens to throw away their cat's favorite toy bunny until they discover the extent of Mog's love and loyalty toward Bunny.
ISBN 0-394-82249-8   ISBN 0-394-92249-2 (lib. bdg.)
[1. Cats—Fiction.]   I. Title.   PZ7.K46815Mn   1989   [E]—dc19   88-16899

One day Mog got a present.
"Here you are, Mog," said Nicky.
"This is for you. It's called Bunny."

Mog liked Bunny.

She carried him about.

She played with him...

and played with him...

and played...

and played...

and played with him.

He was her best thing.

When Mog came to have her supper, Bunny came too.

Sometimes Mog thought Bunny would like a drink.

But Bunny wasn't very good at drinking.
"Oh dear," said Debbie.
"Look where Bunny's gone."

And she put him on the radiator to dry.

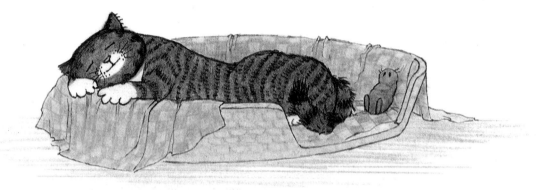

At night Bunny slept with Mog in her basket.

During the day,
when Mog was busy,
she always put Bunny
somewhere nice. You
never knew where
Bunny would go next.

Sometimes Bunny liked to be quiet and cozy,

and sometimes he liked to be where there was a lot happening.

Mr. and Mrs. Thomas didn't understand this.
They didn't say, "Look where Bunny's gone."
They shouted, "Yuk!"

They yelled, "Arrgh! What a horrible, dirty thing!"

And they threatened to throw Bunny away in the trash can.

One day Mr. Thomas said, "Let's have supper in the garden."

Everyone helped to carry things out of the house.

It was a lovely supper.

But suddenly…

there was a crash of thunder and it poured with rain.

"Quick! Inside!" shouted Mrs. Thomas. "It's bedtime anyway."

"Where's Mog?" said Debbie.
"I expect she's keeping dry
under a bush," said Mrs. Thomas.
"She'll come in later."

In the middle of
the night, Debbie
and Nicky woke up.
Mog hadn't come
in and it was still
pouring rain.
"Let's go and find
her," said Debbie.

It was very dark in the garden.
They shouted, "Mog! Where are you, Mog?"
But nothing happened.

Then they heard a meow.

"There she is!" shouted Nicky. "Come on, Mog! Come inside!"

But Mog just went on sitting in the rain.

It was…

dripping…

off her nose.

"What's the matter, Mog?" said Debbie.
Then she said, "Oh dear! Look where Bunny's gone."

Nicky picked Bunny up and showed him to Mog. "It's all right, Mog," he said. "We've set Bunny free. You can come inside now."

Then they carried Bunny through the dark garden…

and through the house...

and they put him on the radiator to dry.

Then they all went to sleep.

In the morning they told Mrs. Thomas what had happened, and how Mog had stayed with Bunny in the dark and the rain.

Debbie said, "You won't really throw Bunny away
in the trash can, will you?"
Mrs. Thomas said, "No, never. It would make Mog too sad."

Then she sighed and said,
"Perhaps he's not quite so
horrible, now he's been washed
by the rain."
They all looked on the radiator.

But this is where Bunny had gone.